SARDINE
in outer space
2

D0052475

SARDINE 2
in outer space
Stories by Emmanuel Guibert
Pictures by Joann Sfar
Color by Walter Pezzali
Translation by Sasha Watson
:01

Contents

Writer: Emmanuel Guibert
Artist: Joann Sfar
The Brainwashing Machine
Today we're going to break into one of Supermuscleman's orphanages and set all your friends free. How do you like that, kids?
Yes!
Yes!
Yes!
Yes!
Yes!
Yes!
Yes!
Yes!
Yes!
Yes!
Yes!
Yes!
Me first!

Meanwhile, at the orphanage ...
We are very honored that you've come to inspect our facilities, great Supermuscleman. You too, Doc Krok.
How is the obedience training progressing, Professor HACKALACK?

Please, you be the judge, great Supermuscleman. This is our brainwashing machine.
WONDERFUL! Which button do I press?

First, press the "Select" key. A child will drop into the machine.
Supermuscle-man, you're a dirty bedpan!
Ew . . . That one was particularly filthy . . .
I'll press "VERY DIRTY"!
This Toxiwash® detergent fluid slowly fills the machine . . .
Krok, you old schmuck!!
Can't we turn off the sound?
Then we rinse the brain and spin it dry . . .
Add a little brain softener to this one!
Click!

There! The child has regained his charming innocence. He is ready to obey.
Who's laughing now, huh?
That'll teach you, you little show-off!
Hack!

I'm very pleased with your work, Professor Hackalack. You'll get a medal for this.
Oh, thank you, great Supermuscleman!
BZZZ
Excuse me, great Supermuscleman. Someone's at the door.
Go ahead! Krok and I are gonna wash another brain.
Yeah!
Click!
BZZZZZ
A medal!
Coming! Coming!
Can I help you?
We're here with the Toxiwash® delivery!

Please be quick, and don't make a mess. The great Supermuscleman is here inspecting the facilities!
No problem! We're pros!
Psshhhh... Hee hee hee!
Hush, Little Louie!
These men are here to refill our Toxiwash® detergent fluid!
Hurry it up!
Hi folks!
All right, kids, you empty out the rest of the Toxiwash® and I'll mix up the replacement fluid.
OK, Uncle Yellow.
Everything OK?
Glugging away!
Glug
Glug
Glug

Bye now, folks!
All done. They're leaving.
Move it!

QUICK! The second part of the plan!
Fill the water guns with the Toxiwash from the machine!
And change your costumes!

What's wrong with this thing, Hackalack? I'm pressing the button, but no kids are coming out . . .
Um . . . There are no more brains left to wash, Supermuscleman!
click! click! click!
click!

There are ALWAYS more brains to wash, Hackalack! Go find one or I'll wash yours instead!
Ri . . . Right away, oh, great Sup . . .
BZZZ

Bzzz
My medal!
It's that blasted doorbell again!
Can I help you?
I'm Professor SCRIBBLESCRABBLE. I've got a new load of kids for you.
Perfect timing! Supermuscleman happens to be here inspecting the facilities. Follow me. And behave yourselves!
No problem! We always do!
Pfsshhh... Hee hee hee!
Hush, Sardine!
Oh Great Supermuscleman, here's a whole classful of brains to wash!
Very good, Hackalack. You can have your medal after all.
Come on, kids! LINE UP!
Clap! Clap!

Supermuscleman, may I suggest that you wash all of their brains at once!
Which button do I press?
Whistle while you work!
Supermuscleman's a jerk!!
Hacka-lack . . .
. . . deserves a smack!
They need deep cleaning! Press all the buttons at once!
Can I press, too?
CLIC CLICK CLICK CLICK CLICK CLIC CLICK CLIC CLICK CLIC CLICK CLIC CLICK
Don't worry, guys, drink up. It's not Toxiwash®, it's pink lemonade!

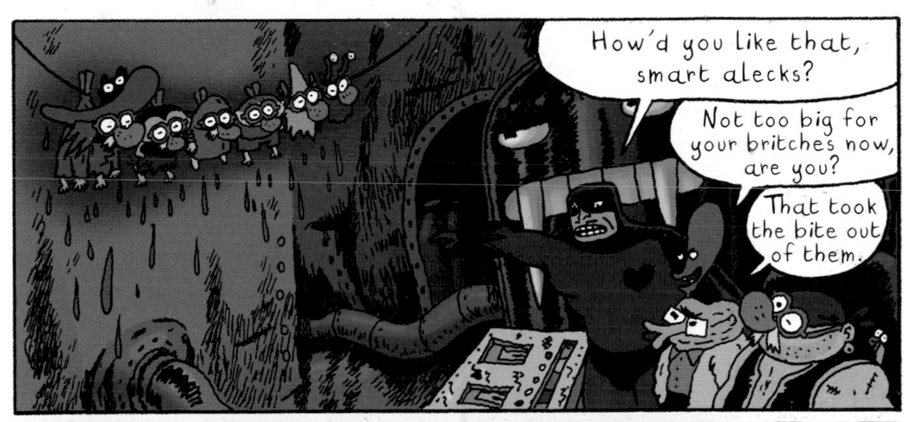
How'd you like that, smart alecks?
Not too big for your britches now, are you?
That took the bite out of them.

You think so?

Guess what's in our water guns, Supermuscleman!
YELLOW SHOULDER! YOU MUTINEER!

Your favorite, Toxiwash®!

Later on ...
We did it, Uncle Yellow! All the kids are aboard the Huckleberry and the effects of the Toxiwash® are starting to wear off!
And we've recovered our lemonade!
MISSION ACCOMPLISHED!

Doesn't look like the brainwashing machine is doing anything . . .
Guys this dumb need triple-washing, Sardine!
THE END!

Writer: Emmanuel Guibert
Artist: Joann Sfar
The Cha-Cha Fly
IF YOU'RE HERE TO STAY LET'S DANCE THE NIGHT AWAY
Do you hear shouting?
That's not shouting, Uncle Yellow. Someone's singing a song.

Singing? In the middle of the jungle?
It is pretty weird.
Could we go back to the ship? We have some nice music there.
I LIKE HOW YOU MOVE WHEN WE'RE IN THE GROOVE
It's coming from over there. Let's go see!
I hate this planet, Sardine!
Don't you like the jungle beat, Little Louie?
YEAH, YOU'RE IN THE GROOVE AND I FEEL SO SMOOTH
OH! Poor thing!!
I know how to shut him up, Uncle Yellow!

No, Sardine, you don't understand. This poor guy's been bitten by a CHA-CHA fly.
A Cha-Cha fly?
CHA, CHA, CHACHACHA I LIKE YOUR GROOVE
The Cha-Cha fly has a terrible bite, kids.
Does it itch a lot?
AND YOU LIKE MY GROOVE AND YOU ARE SO SMOOTH
No, Little Louie, it's much worse! Once you've been bitten, you get stupid dance tunes stuck in your head and you can't get them out!
AND YOU LIKE MY GROOVE CUZ I AM SO SMOOTH
And this one's skipping on top of it. Where's that club, Sardine?
Here, Uncle Yellow.

OOH I LIKE YOUR
BAM!
AAH!
There . . . Now he'll rest for a few minutes.
And so will we!
YUM! Come look!
Look–crunch!–someone dropped a whole bunch of chocolate truffles! . . . YUM!
Those aren't truffles, they're Cha-Cha fly turds!
BLECK! YUCK!
HA! HA! HA!
Cha-Cha flies live in cocoa trees. They use their delicious chocolate turds to lure their victims to them.
Gross! But delicious . . .

Hello, BRITNEY and CHRISTINA? This is JUSTIN and CLAY. We have three intruders in our sector. What do you say?
Wait for us, boys, we're on our way!
BZ...
BZZZ...
It was a bad idea to have a picnic on Planet Ouchypoo. It's too dangerous. Let's get back to the ship, fast!
I'll hold onto this club in case he wakes up, Uncle Yellow.
CRUNCH MUNCH MUNCH
BZZZ!
CAPTAIN! IT'S THE CHOCOLATE FLIES!
Ha ha! We'll vaccinate you!
We'll fill your little head with pretty music...
BZZZ
BZZZ
BZZZ
...Fill it till it bursts! Ha ha!
ZZZZ
You guys ready? I wanna sting!
BZZZ

Little Louie . . . Do you still have that glue gun? Now's your chance to use it!
Smart!
BANZZZAI!
ZZZ
ZZZZ
ZZZZ
Splurch!
BZZT!
Stick!
Stick!
BZT!
ZZZZ
Good job, Little Louie! That was a bull's-eye!
WATCH OUT! There are two more!

SMAK!
There goes one!
squish!
SWEET REVENGE!
HEY, get outta here, you nasty bugger!!
AAAAH!
Sting!
TWO DOWN! Those Cha-Cha flies won't sting again!
CHA CHA, CHACHA-CHA
Here, Uncle Yellow.

Whack!
It's too bad those flies sting 'cause they make really good chocolate. Want one?
Just a taste.
BZ
BZ
H ...hello, STING? The intruders have decimated our squadron...
Hello, this is Sting. I'm sending reinforcements.
Let's get out of here! There might be more!
Are you sure it's this way, Uncle Yellow?
We should have left a trail of crumbs or something, to keep us from getting lost.
There's the Huckle . . . OH NO!!

It's covered with Cha-Cha flies!
We're done for!
BZZZZZ

No, look! They aren't moving!
BZT
BZT
BZT
HA! HA! HA! I get it!!
They were planning an ambush but the Huckleberry is so filthy that they got stuck!
Let's go wash them off. There's a waterfall right nearby.
BZT

OOH I LIKE YOUR GROOVE MAKE ME FEEL SO SMOOTH
Uncle Yellow, why are you letting him sing that stupid song?
Oh, everyone sings in the shower, Sardine!
BZZT! Please!
HELP!
Rescue me!
CHA CHA, CHACHA . . .
BAM!
There! That's the end of it. Good-bye, Planet Ouchypoo!
You know what, Louie? We should have kept one of those flies to make chocolate for us.
I tried, Sardine, but it just got away.
The END

Writer: Emmanuel Guibert
Artist: Joann Sfar
Merry Christmas, Supermuscleman!
Is that you, Captain Yellow Shoulder? I'm here to drop off the presents . . .
Sardine! Little Louie! It's Santa Claus!
NOEL EXPRESS

Don't bother waking the kids. Just give 'em this for me.
That's it?
Yup! See you next year!
Wait one minute . . .
You've got a rocket ship stuffed full of presents and all you're giving me is this little trinket?
You gotta have cash if you want the good ones.
OH YEAH?!
YEAH!

Later . . .
Wake up, kids! It's Christmas!
We weren't sleeping! We waited up all night!
Snore ...
Where'd you get that costume, Uncle Yellow?
This guy loaned it to me.
Everything in here is for you. Pick whatever you want. And no fighting!
Yay!
First dibs!

Hey, Captain, is this some kind of joke?
WHAT?!
You know who these are for?!
I told you, they're for you!
NO! They're all for Supermuscleman.
They are? Let me see . . .
Supermuscleman
Supermuscleman
er muscleman
A stink bomb!
Pollution powder!
A do-it-yourself torture rack!
Blimey! What're we gonna do with all this stuff?
Heeheehee! We should deliver it to Supermuscleman ourselves!

Meanwhile, in outer space...
I don't understand, Krok. He should have been here hours ago. Do you think he forgot about me?
Don't worry, Supermuscleman. Here, put on your robe. It's getting chilly.
Do you think he came and we didn't hear him? Maybe he thought no one was home so he left.
No, he would've drunk the hot chocolate you left out for him. The cup's still full!
SM
Maybe he just doesn't like me anymore.
Knock! Knock! Knock!
KROK! THAT'S HIM!!
There he is!

WAAAH!
What now?
NO ONE'S THERE!
But wait! Look!
His cup is empty. He did come!
Then where are my presents?
Your presents? Well . . . There they are.
Are you kidding?!
A pair of baby scissors, a thimble, and a key chain?!! I asked for WEAPONS, Krok!!
Santa Claus is coming . . .

Were you good this year?

Merry Christmas.
YIPPEE!
VINCE
DECAPITATORRR!
STAN
DECAPITATORRR!

Look, Krok! I love it!
Don't hurt yourself, Supermuscleman!
Can I light the tree now, Uncle Yellow?
Go ahead.
ORRR
Zzzzzzt...
MERRY CHRISTMAS, SUPERMUSCLEMAN AND DOC KROK!!
SLAM!

BANG
ZAP!
RATATATAT!
ZIIIIIP
ZAP!
Ouch!
Eeeeek!
Thanks for the cool fireworks display, Uncle Yellow! MWAH!
Thanks, Captain! MWAH!
HA HA HA! Call me SANTA CLAUS, kids!
The END

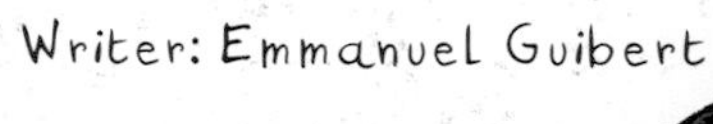

Writer: Emmanuel Guibert

Artist: Joann Sfar

Bobby Bigmouth

Hey, you geese! Where are you headed?
We're going to feed BOBBY BIGMOUTH.
Who's Bobby Bigmouth?
He's a monster!
If we don't bring him lots of good stuff to eat on New Year's Eve, he devours everything in sight for the whole year.
No kidding!

What a disgusting monster!
Let's ruin his appetite!
I'll call Grammy to tell her we'll be a little late for New Year's dinner!
beep beep beep
I didn't tell Grammy that we're chasing after a big monster. She'd be worried if she knew.
Very good, Little Louie.
HELLO, HELLO . . . Calling all geese . . . We're approaching our target . . . Prepare for airdrop . . .

LOOK! There's Bobby Bigmouth!
SCARY!

The geese are dropping their cargo into his mouth.
Hooooooonk
Let's get a closer look!
SNAP!

It's dark inside Bobby Bigmouth!
He shut his mouth.
I think I see a light over there ...
Champagne! Caviar! Oysters! Tons and tons of them!
We must be in his stomach.
Ooh, I wish it was French fries, cake, and strawberry milkshakes!
That'd be an awesome New Year, Sardine!
PEOPLE! FINALLY! Welcome, welcome!
?
?

Who are you?
I'm Bobby!
Gimme a kiss!
Splsssh
Are you really Bobby?
I'm Bobby and this is my ship, the INSATIABLE.
He's so tiny!
I'm a very lonely little worm. In fact, I was so starved for affection that I built this big-mouth ship so I could give giant kisses!

So you'd stop causing trouble for the universe if you had some friends?

Yes, that's all I want!

Here's what you're going to do: give away your caviar, your champagne, and your oysters to anyone in the galaxy who doesn't have any of their own. And SMILE while you do it!
OK.
When you're done, you can come find us at our Grammy's house. We'll save some cake for you.
GREAT! I'LL write down the address!
Later, at Grammy's house . . .
That's the doorbell!
It must be Bobby!
Let's go see.

You were right! I made lots of friends when I gave all that stuff away! I even found a girlfriend!
HA! That's wonderful!
Allow me to introduce TEENA.
I told you so.
HAPPY NEW YEAR, EVERYONE!
Happy New Year, Sardine!
Happy New Year, Bobby!
Happy New Year, Little Louie!
Happy New Year, Grammy!
Happy New Year, Teena!
Happy New Year, Pokemon!
Happy New Year, Uncle Yellow!
Happy New Year, Captain!
Happy New Year!
HAPPY NEW YEAR!
The End

Writer: Emmanuel Guibert
Artist: Joann Sfar
The Mix-and-Mingle Suit
SUPERMUSCLEMAN
Want to go, kids?
Ooh, yes, Captain! Let's go!
Town Hall Meeting-- TONIGHT!
We promise not to be good!

Meanwhile . . .
Supermuscleman, you have to mix and mingle after your speech tonight.
AGAIN?! I already did, just last week!
I made you a special mix-and-mingle suit. Here, try it on.
I hate to mix and mingle.
What are all these hands for? I look like a centipede!
They'll help you wade through the crowd without getting tired.
Here's the remote control. . .
You try out your new suit. I have to go write your speech now.
OK, I'll see you later.

Later that night . . .

I want to talk to you ...
I . . . ?
You want to talk to me, Doc Krok?
No, dingbat! You want to talk to them!
OH! I . . . YEAH! I'm the one that wants to talk to them . . . uh, I mean . . . you!
Boy oh boy...
Boy oh boy ...
What a moron!!
This guy is too much!

Tell me, Sir, what do you find so great about President Supermuscle-man?
The President? He's the best!
He's really strong!
And he's so handsome, too!
PRESIDENT SUPERMUSCLEMAN
Don't you think he's pretty stup . .
Look! The President's going to mix and mingle!
PRESIDENT SUPERMUSCLEMAN
Don't push, Doc Krok!
Don't worry, Super-muscleman. I'm right here with you.

Why's he wearing that strange belt?
?
Heehee! That gives me an idea, Little Louie . . . Get your glue gun!
See Doc Krok's remote control? . . . Get it for me!
Sweet!
Thanks to your mix-and-mingle suit, Supermuscleman, you can shake hands without actually touching anyone!
You're right, it's very practical.
?
HEY!
Sploosh!

I got it!
You rock, Little Louie!
Uncle Yellow, take the remote control. I want Supermuscleman to punch as many people as he can!
Got it!
We're going to the podium! Come on, Little Louie!
Can I talk into the microphone?
SUPE
Uh . . . Doc Krok? I don't want to mix and mingle anymore!
AARGH! Someone stole my remote control!

SMACK!
SMACK!
SMACK!
SMACK!
Ouch!
Eee!
SMACK!
Ooph!
Waah!
SMACK!
SMACK!
OUCH!
HA HA HA! Supermuscleman, your approval ratings are going down!
The president just punched me!
Me too! He's really strong!!
SMM
SUPERMUSCLEMAN! Stop your arms!
I don't like this! I want out!!
SMACK!
SMACK!
SMACK!
SMACK!
Ouch!
SMACK!
Ouch!
SMACK!
SMACK!
SMACK!
SMACK!
Eeeh!
SMACK!
SMACK!
Oooph!

Give me the mike!
I get one, too!
HELLO EVERYONE! This is SARDINE FROM OUTER SPACE talking!
AND LITTLE LOUIE!
ARE YOU TIRED OF GETTING PUNCHED IN THE FACE BY PRESIDENT SUPERMUSCLEMAN?
SARDINE! Wait'll I get my hands on you!
AND GETTING YOUR EARS BOXED?
?
?
?
?
SMACK!
Yeah, I am tired of it!
We clap for him and he beats us up!
It's an outrage!
DOWN WITH SUPER-MUSCLEMAN!

DOC KROK! THEY'RE SURROUNDING ME!
KEEP PUNCHING THEM! KEEP PUNCHING THEM!

ANY TIME YOU DECIDE TO GO MIXING AND MINGLING, SUPERMUSCLEMAN, LET SARDINE LEND A HAND!
SMACK!
SMACK!
SMACK!
OUCH!
SMACK!
SMACK!
SMACK!
SMACK!
Ha! Ha!
Ha!
Ha!
Ha!
Ha!
Ha!
Ha!
Ha! Ha!
Ha!
Ha!
Ha Ha!
Ha!
The End!

Writer: Emmanuel Guibert
Artist: Joann Sfar
Ava Garbo
Hello, children. Put your hands in the air, please. This is a stickup.
Wait a minute. We have to tell our captain.
?

Uncle Yellow, there's an old man here who wants to rob us.
Er . . . yes, well, I don't want to disturb you but . . .
You're not much of a robber!
SNIFF! I'll never be able to do it!
Heeeee haaw!
Come on, come on! Sit down, have a drink, and tell us all about it.
Thank you. Sniff . . .

Well . . . My name is Andy and I live on a little satellite that orbits the space star Follywood. The great actress AVA GARBO lives on Follywood. Do you know who she is?
Never heard of her.

Ah, it was before your time. People were crazy about her in the old days. Her star used to shine brighter than all the others.

But she never leaves her big Follywood mansion anymore. Everyone's forgotten all about her except for me!
That's so sad.

Now Follywood's light is growing dim, and soon it will be cold and gray if I don't do something about it!
So, why'd you try to rob us?

I . . . I want to plate Follywood with gold. Then it will shine just as brightly as before, and Ava Garbo will love me!
Well, you came to the wrong place. We're broke!

You know who has lots of gold? Supermuscleman!
Oh, I could never rob Supermuscleman!
I bet we could!
YEAH! Like in the movies!
LATER ON, FAR AWAY...
Good news, Supermuscleman sir. You just keep getting richer!
How much have I got, Doc Krok?

You have so much gold that I can't even count it all, and there isn't enough room for it on the ship!

Let's buy some weapons and start a war!

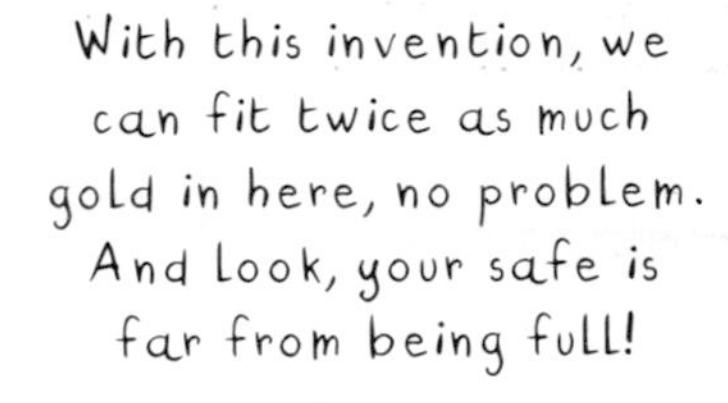

In fact, it's totally empty!
WHAT?!
We've been robbed!!
And they signed their names!
Yellow Shoulder
SARDINE
LITTLE LOUIE
EVEN LATER, AND EVEN FARTHER AWAY...
What luck!
I've never written my name in gold letters before.
Aw, it's just like the frosting Grammy uses to decorate her cakes, except with gold instead of sugar.
Grammy's frosting tastes a lot better!

Now it'll be easy to plate Follywood with gold. Just squeeze out these tubes and spread it on!
We're here!
What a depressing star!
Land here, Captain.
AND AFTER A FEW HOURS OF WORK . . .
Gee, that was tough going!
It's so shiny!
My friends, how can I ever thank you!

Follywood is shiny and bright, just like the good old days! Ava Garbo will be so happy!
Go find her!
I'm nervous! I've waited light-years for this moment!
Don't worry, she'll love it!
DING DONG
Does my spacesuit look silly?
You look like a movie star!
Yes? Can I help you?
Uh... Hello, Madame... We're here to see the divine Ava Garbo...

Ava Garbo? Why, she hasn't lived here for years! My name is Janine.
Ja...Janine?

What the heck did you do to my star? It's much too bright! I'm old, you know, and my eyes are tired!
Er . . . I thought . . . I mean . . .

Mister Andy thought you were tired of living in this big mansion all by yourself.

So he wants to invite you to come live with him on his little satellite. It'll be perfect for the two of you. Right, Mister Andy?
Er . . . well, I mean . . . yes . . .

And Follywood will shine down on you in your golden years!
Do you have a TV?
Yes! And I have a DVD player and all of Ava Garbo's movies!
Oh, well, all right then. I'll go with you.
That's great, Janine! I promise you won't regret it!
Ava Garbo has changed a lot but her little dog looks just the same.
WHAT?! Janine is Ava Garbo? We have to tell Mister Andy!
Forget it, Little Louie! They're happy just the way they are!
The End

Writer: Emmanuel Guibert
Artist: Joann Sfar
Dunderhead
The Flea circus
YAY!
Isn't this a great show, Uncle Yellow?
It's fantastic!
CLAP! CLAP!

The flea circus would like to thank Yellow Shoulder, Sardine, and Little Louie for coming out . . .
WATCH OUT!
WATCH OUT! IT'S DUNDER-HEAD!
Oh, no!
EVERYONE HIDE!! THERE'S A DUNDERHEAD COMING!
What's a Dunderhead, Uncle Yellow Shoulder?
Let's go and see . . .

A GIANT!!
BOOM!
The Flea Circus
HELP US!!
RUN FOR YOUR LIVES!!

He's crushing the big top!
CRRACK!
WHAT THE?! That beanpole ought to look where he's going!
Hurry, Little Louie! Those fleas need our help!

LATER ...
The FLEA circus is ruined! SOB!
Come now, Mr. Fleabag. At least no one was killed, that's what counts!
We'll help you build an even better big top.
BAH! What's the point? That Dunderhead always wrecks everything!
He has no respect!
All that Dunderhead thinks about is himself!
Chin up, people! If you fix up the FLEA circus, we'll take care of Dunderhead!
Yeah! We've demolished guys bigger than him!

A LITTLE LATER...
There he is!
Why is he always staring at his hands like that?
He must be counting something.
ZZZ...
SNRRR
BAM!
He's asleep.
He was counting sheep!
Come on, let's go look!

Look, Uncle Yellow! He has televisions where his fingernails should be.
SNRRR
Televisions?
What's he watching?
It looks like tunnels and caves!
No wonder he fell asleep!
I know what it is!
CLAP!
Remember what that flea said? "All that Dunderhead thinks about is himself!"
These televisions show the INSIDE OF DUNDERHEAD!

I have an idea, but first we have to get inside Dunderhead.
Let's find a hole!
Uh . . . You'll have better luck looking up by his face.
THIS WAY, SARDINE! HIS BELLYBUTTON COMES OFF!
You're too big, Uncle Yellow. We'll be right back!
I'll watch you on TV.
His body must be full of video cameras, Little Louie! And I want every one of them pointing at us.
EASY! All we have to do is play soccer!

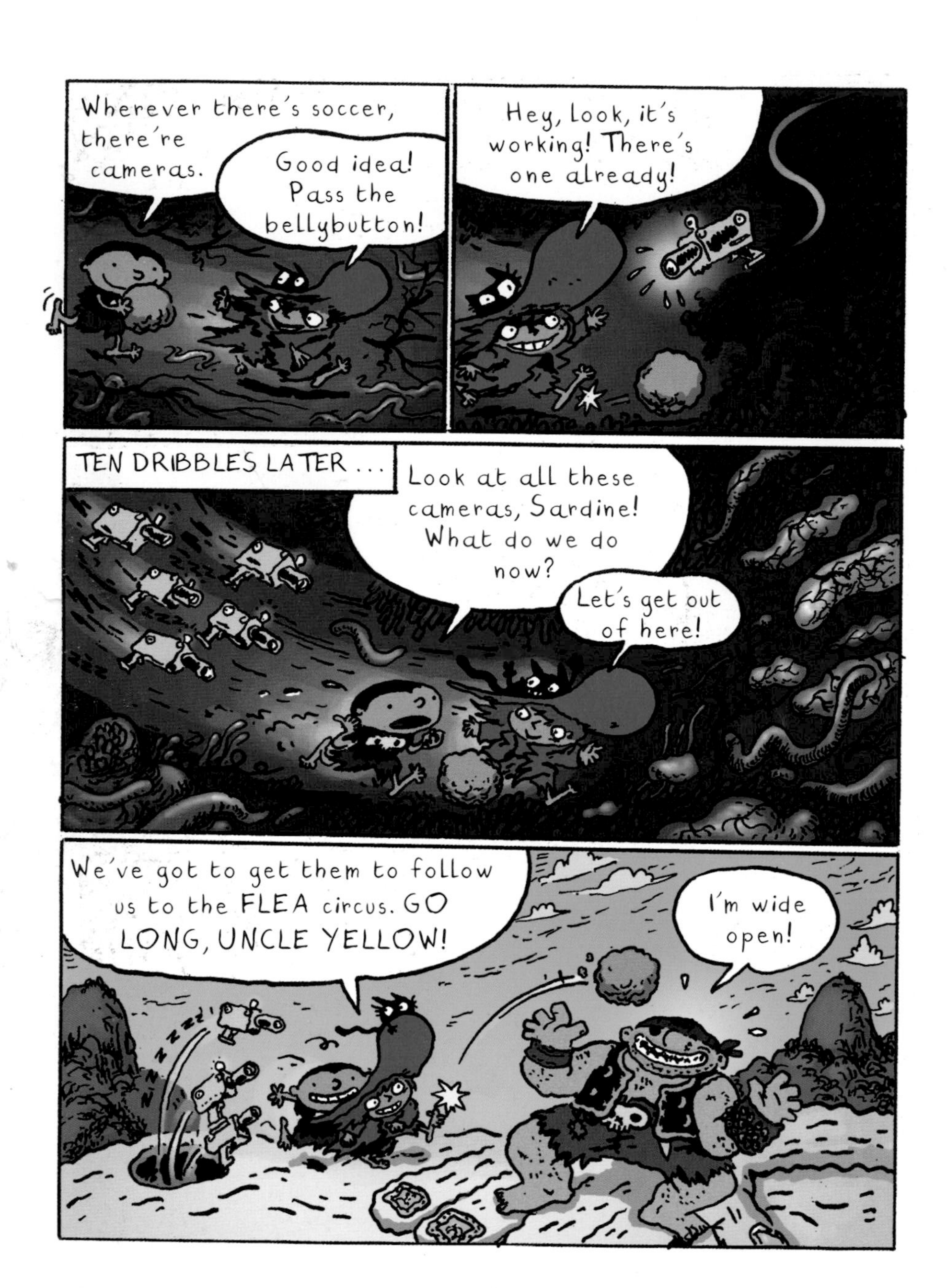
Wherever there's soccer, there're cameras.
Good idea! Pass the bellybutton!
Hey, look, it's working! There's one already!
TEN DRIBBLES LATER ...
Look at all these cameras, Sardine! What do we do now?
Let's get out of here!
We've got to get them to follow us to the FLEA circus. GO LONG, UNCLE YELLOW!
I'm wide open!

AT THE FLEA CIRCUS . . .
I've got it!
Hey, Mr. Fleabag! Start the show! We brought you an audience!
But, but, but . . . The big top's not ready!
It doesn't matter! Just do something funny for us!
Portia! Portabello! Portapotty! The show must go on!
YES, BOSS!
Dunderhead is waking up . . .
If everything goes right, he'll see the flea circus in his fingernails.
I hope he likes it!

HAHAHA
He likes it!
HAHAHAHAHA
As long as you keep him entertained, Mr. Fleabag, he'll leave you in peace!
Thank you, Sardine. We couldn't ask for more.
I'm keeping his bellybutton as a souvenir!
GOAL!

Writer: Emmanuel Guibert
Artist: Joann Sfar
By the Light of Big Ursa Bear
HEY! BIG URSA BEAR!!
YELLOW SHOULDER, YOU OLD PIRATE! Drop your anchor and come in for a drink!

What wind blows you this way, you old swashbuckler?
We saw the light on so we came on over! HA HA!
BIG URSA'S LIGHTHOUSE
Sardine and Louie, this is Big Ursa Bear, the best lighthouse keeper in the whole galaxy.
Hello, Ma'am!
They're adorable! Let me call my daughter...
LITTLE URSA BEAR! We have guests! Come down and say hello!
Leave me alone!
COMMANDO FADA
LEE PERRY
ROOTS
No Blood for Oil!
CHOUPM
QUESTION AUTHORITY
Reggaetón!

Little Ursa Bear, you come out of this room right now before I drag you out!
But, MOOOOM! I'm working!
Reggae Gold 2005
Sister Nancy
deebee beedee
Rabbit
I AM
GERM WARFARE
WU TANG
Heh heh . . . Hi there, Little Ursa Bear . . . You're a lot taller than the last time I saw you!
Yeah, well, you're older and fatter.
Do you hear how she talks to grownups?
We'll be worse than that when we're her age!
Listen to me! You're going to be polite and show Sardine and Louie around the lighthouse while Yellow Shoulder and I sit and talk.
GRRR!

She's not very friendly, is she?
HA HA! She'll get over it! Come have a drink!
So are you gonna show us the lighthouse?
Does it say NANNY BEAR on my forehead or what?
No, but it does say TEDDY BEAR . . .
. . . And we don't play with teddy bears!
Hey, chill, little fellas! We're all brothers and sisters, right?
Step on it!
Keep it moving!

You've gotta understand. I don't have anything against you, I'm just so bored in this lighthouse!
Have you tried sliding down the banisters?

Yeah, like a million times. It's no fun anymore. You space pirates are so lucky—you get to travel all over the universe!
Yeah, we are!

I'm pretty lonely here. My mom's all right, but the lighthouse takes up all her time.
That's sad . . .
I have an idea!
STUPID LIGHTHOUSE!

MEANWHILE, DEEP IN SPACE ...
We're approaching planet BUBULINA, Supermuscleman, Sir!
I can't wait to get home! First, I'll visit my palace, then my prisons, then my barracks...
AAH!
What?
QUAKE 1000
TH... THERE'S A GIANT SARDINE ON PLANET BUBULINA!!
A giant sardine? Did you smoke something funny, Doc Krok?

Was this a great idea or what?
I never thought of making shadow puppets on planets before!
My turn, Sardine!
Now there's a giant Little Louie! Do you see it?
OH, THE SWINE!! But he ...
HE'S PEEING ON BUBULINA!
You're disgusting, Little Louie!
Whaddaya mean?
ZIP!
HA HA! Good one! Now it's my turn!

HORRORS!
BUBULINA JUST VANISHED!
Shoot! You can't see anything!
You're too big, Little Ursa Bear. You're casting a shadow over the whole planet.
Just make one with your hand!
Okay . . . guess what this is!
BANG!

Oh, cool! It's a gun!
Bang?
Put it right in the middle, Little Ursa Bear!
Look, it's magic! The gun's smoking!
But BUBULINA disappeared . . . I saw it!
Oh, forget it, Doc Krok . . . It's good to be home!

LATER . . .

Did you have fun, kids?
Yeah, Mom, we did! Sardine and Louie are really cool!
Can we come back soon, Uncle Yellow?
Of courshe we can, Schlardine...
Did you have fun, too, Captain?
Me?
I think I had too much to drink. I just saw a planet wave good-bye . . .
The End

Writer: Emmanuel Guibert
Artist: Joann Sfar
103° Fahrenheit
What's wrong with Sardine?
She has a fever, Little Louie. Come on, let's make her a nice cup of tea with honey.

MEANWHILE, ON PLANETBUBULINA ...
Channel 103
103 fm
Tonight is HOT HOTHOT on 103 FM!

103 FM, your number one station for shivers, shakes, aches, and pains . . .
103 fm
And runny noses!

And now, a little music for Sardine!

AAAH!

Supermuscleman, take off your head-phones!
Wha . . . what was that music?

It's a one-man band! He can hit a pan with a fork, grind his teeth, snort like a pig, and crack his knuckles, all at once.
It's awful . . .

Sardine will really hate it!
And that's not all! Follow me . . .

Krok, this plan to poison Sardine's dreams is absolutely perfect!
Heh heh!

These are the Channel 103 TV studios, Supermuscleman!
THE TELEVIRUS!

Here we have ridiculous monsters in a hideous set, engaging in absurd and repetitive battles!
Don't you think Sardine might like that?

No way! But, like the radio program, it will fill her thoughts, worry her...
...AND MAKE HER SICK!
Take this space ogre ... Right now, Sardine is dreaming that he's about to eat her...
...And she can't fight back!
RROAAARR

GROOWL!
ARF!
HISSSSSSSS!
Where'd that cat come from?
That's Sardine's cat!
How'd he get in here?
That filthy animal sneaks in everywhere! We've got to catch it!
He's leaving the studio!
CUT! Stop the cameras!!
103 TV apologizes for this temporary break in programming . . .
Mmm . . .

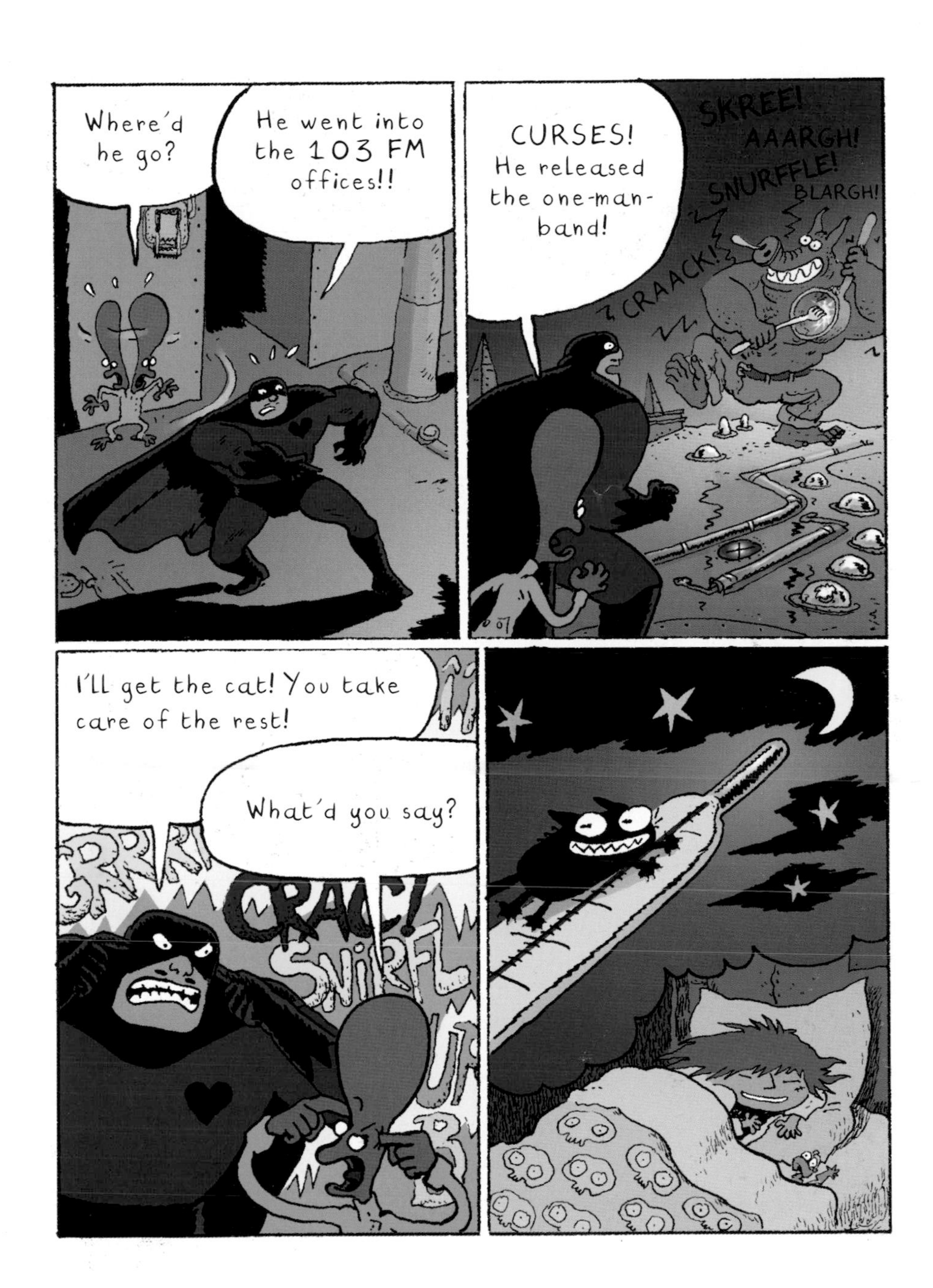

Where'd he go?
He went into the 103 FM offices!!
CURSES! He released the one-man-band!
SKREE!
AAARGH!
SNURFFLE!
BLARGH!
CRAACK!
CRAACK
I'll get the cat! You take care of the rest!
What'd you say?
GRRR
CRAC!
SNIRFL

He's climbing up the antenna! I'll corner him . . .
What'd you say?
SNORFFLE!
EEK!
SKREEK!
RFFLE
Doc Krok, stop following me! You'll break the antenna.
Don't go any further, Supermuscleman! You'll break the antenna!
SNORFFLE!
SKRE
SKREEK!
SKREEK!
SNOR
SNORFFLE

Here, kitty kitty . . .
Get back to work, all of you! This is a live broadcast!
AAARGH!
BLARGH!
SKREE!
SNURFFLE!
SNORT
CRAACK!
Hee hee
ha hee ha

AAAAH!
Here, Sardine, drink this lemon tea!
Lemon tea? How come?
Well...because you have a fever...
Not anymore I don't! I want ice cream!...
...and lots of kitty treats. He really deserves them!
MRRR...

I had the craziest dream. Supermuscleman and Doc Krok were there . . .
They're the ones who deserve to get sick!
Yum
yum
SLURP
SLURP
Gulp
Scratch
103 fM
We're sunk, Doc Krok!
What? What'd you say?
SNURFFLE!
SKREE!
AAARGH!
Kling
Klang
bubu
Snap
CRAACK!
BLARGH!
snort
snoot
Bzzzzt
The End

Writer: Emmanuel Guibert
Artist: Joann Sfar
Zargon and the Zargonites
That planet has land and water! Can we stop here, Uncle Yellow?
HA! HA! HA! You're in for a surprise!
Café de l'espace

Are you crazy, Captain? You're landing in the middle of the ocean!
Put on your floatie, Little Louie!
Wowzers! It's blue like the ocean, but it's not the ocean!
Heh heh . . . I got you good that time!
?
This is carpet!
Yup! We're on the carpet comet.
The whole thing is covered with carp . . .
Welcome to ZARGONIA, strangers!

I am the Emperor ZARGON the First and these are my people, the ZARGONITES.
GNAP!
GNAP!
GNAP!
GNAP!

You've come to buy a carpet, I presume?
Oh, no, not at all. We're just looking.
GNAP!
GNAP!
GNAP!

Here we have the Great Book of Sacred Samples. Go ahead and pick your color.
GNAP!
GNAP!
GNAP!
GNAP!

White is nice but I wouldn't advise it for anyone with children. The mustard yellow goes with everything, and I just love this shade of apricot . . .
WAIT A MINUTE!
GNAP!
GNAP!

We're not interested in buying a carpet right now. We don't have anywhere to put it, anyway.
How about inside your ship?
It's a pirate ship! Who ever saw a carpeted pirate ship!
Might I tempt you with a nice black carpet with a skull and crossbones design?
GNAP!
GNAP!
GNAP!
WE-ARE-NOT-INTERESTED, got me? Now, BEAT IT!
Oh, it's like that, is it?!
GNAP!
GNAP!
GNAP!
GNAP!
GNAP!
A terrible vengeance will be wrought upon you! Thus speaks Zargon!
Yeah, yeah . . . Later, dude!

You know, Uncle Yellow, it would be nice to have a carpet . . . at least in our bedroom.
I said NO, Sardine!
Well, can we sleep on this blue carpet tonight, anyway?
Ooh, can we, Captain? It's so fluffy and soft!
Weeeell . . . All right. We'll leave in the morning.
Sleep tight, kids. I'll keep one eye open in case Zargon tries any funny business.
Make sure it's your good eye, Uncle Yellow!
If I catch Zargon the First, I'll crush him between my little toes!

THE NEXT MORNING AT DAWN...
Little Louie, wake up! Uncle Yellow's gone!
Hmph?
I've looked everywhere, I've called for him . . . but he doesn't answer! The Zargonites must have kidnapped him!
Really? How'd they do it?
Scrtch! Scrtch!
!
It doesn't matter! Come on! We need equipment so we can exterminate those little bugs!
We have lots of weapons for fighting big monsters, but there's nothing for microbes!
I have an idea!
SNAP!
MEANWHILE . . .
Where in space am I?
HA!HA!
GNAP!
GNAP!
GNAP!
GNAP! GNAP!

All right, Mr. Pirate! What do you say now?
ZARGON! Are you still trying to sell me that old carpet?!
GNAP!
GNAP!
GNAP!
TOO LATE! You have committed a grave offense and you must pay! I leave you to my cruel Zargonites!
Enjoy your dinner, my pretties!
LONG LIVE ZARGON THE FIRST!
LONG LIVE THE EMPEROR!!

MEANWHILE . . .
That way, Sardine! There's some kind of building!
It must be their base. ATTACK!
VRRRRRRRRRR
SPACE CARPETS FOR SALE
Oh Great Zargon! There's a frightful machine coming straight at us!
Later! Not while I'm eating!
Munch!
Munch!
Start the VACUUM CLEANER, Little Louie!
Vacuum on!
Click!
AAH!
CLOSE THE DOOR! There's a draft!
HELP!

HA! HA! We're gobbling them up, Little Louie!
I never knew vacuuming could be so much fun!
AAAH!
Hey, Uncle Yellow! You were up against the wall, huh?
The wall-to-wall! Ha!
Snip!
Look! Zargon escaped from the vacuum cleaner!
HAVE PITY! I ... I have a family to feed!
Don't worry, Zargon! We're not gonna hurt you! We just want to straighten up your empire a little . . .
What do you mean? ...
Put the vacuum on the razor setting, Little Louie!
Razor on!
click!

MY CARPET! SHE'S SHAVING MY BEAUTIFUL CARPET!!
That'll teach you to eat your guests, Zargon!
VROOM!

Poor Zargon! We only left him a tiny island of carpet!
It's funny—there was a nice hardwood floor underneath all that!
I swiped a few pieces of the pirate carpet. Let's go put them in our room, Little Louie!
The End

Writer: Emmanuel Guibert
Artist: Joann Sfar
The Yogurt Thieves
Little Louie, are you sleeping?
ASTERPEEKS
the COW BOY
POP
The Schmlurfs
Nrrr . . .
Devil by Night
Devil by Day
DD
H

Did you say NRRR or NO?
YZZZ...
Did you say YZZZ or YES?
NRRR ...
Go ahead and sleep then, you baby! I'm going for a walk!
YZZZ...
It's so annoying that Little Louie is always asleep when I'm not even tired!
Rrrow...
Uncle Yellow, too. He snores so loudly!
SNORRGG
Peter Pan
zzz

You know what, kitty? Since no one wants to play with us, we're gonna have a nice glass of milk.
Myum!
GALLOPING GALAXIES! The fridge is empty!
BOOM! BOOM!
And there's someone in the freezer!
A white lady!
MMMPH . . . MMMPH!

Are you the Snow Queen?
I'll explain later. Untie me, quickly!
Where are you taking us?
I'm going after those fridge looters! Buckle up!
WOW!
I didn't know we had a refrigerocket!
It's an old model with a manual defroster. It should really be replaced.

Who are you anyway?
I'm the Ice Watcher. I'm the one who keeps an eye on your ice cream and space yogurt while you're sleeping.
Not long ago, two guys broke into the fridge. They took me by surprise, tied me up, and stole all your dairy products before escaping.
Ah! What pigs!
We'll get them, though! Their ship must have a leak—it's leaving a trail of milk behind. All we have to do is follow it.
What a waste! With all the little aliens who are starving!

MEANWHILE . . .
Milk, yogurt, cheese, ice cream, pudding . . . We really hit the jackpot this time, Doc Krok!
Hee Hee Hee! Those kids won't get big and strong now, Supermuscleman!
"Astrofruit on the Bottom." YUM! I love these!
SLURP
Another milk bottle stolen from the mouth of a babe!
We're approaching the Milky Way. We'll dump our booty here and then go back for more.
TOLL
Have you checked your expiration date?
Now entering THE MILKY WAY
Got fuel?
Welcome to the Milk Turnpike

Supermuscleman is approaching. Raise the gate.
I read you. Raising the gate.

The empire of milk is yours, Supermuscleman. These toll booths guarantee you money and power!
Bleeech . . . I think I ate too much condensed milk. . .

ALERT! ALERT! UNIDENTIFIED VEHICLE! LOWER THE GATE!
Ping! Ping! Ping!
I read you. Lowering the gate.
Ping! Ping! Ping!

CRACK!
Ping! Ping! Ping! Ping!
We break it, we take it!
A refrigerocket is shooting ice cubes at us!
PAM! PAM!
Doc Krok, pull over . . . I don't feel good . . .
That's Supermuscleman and Doc Krok's space-bat! Slam into it, Ice Watcher!
That's strange . . .
They're heading straight into a turn. I don't think they see it!
Doc Krok, I'm gonna be siiiiiiick!
Ping! Ping! Ping! Ping! Ping!
SUPERMUSCLEMAN, LET GO OF THE CONTROLS!

AAAHH!!
THE MILK! IT'S TURNING!

KA-PLOSH
Barf!

LATER . . .
You like tying people up, HUH?! Well, now it's your turn!!
GRR!
Let's go, Sardine! We'll take a spin around the Milky Way and get rid of all those awful toll booths. No one should have to pay for milk!

Doc Krok, I'm getting freezer burn!
Obviously! That awful Sardine put us in the deep-freeze! If only being full of hot air could get us out of this cold spell!
THE NEXT MORNING . . .
ATCHOO!
ATCHOO!
That's funny—the fridge has a cold!
Hey, Sardine, I don't remember buying all these yogurts!
I couldn't sleep last night, so I went yogurt shopping!
The End

Writer: Emmanuel Guibert
Artist: Joann Sfar
Gone Fish-ishing
Pu-pull in the ne-nets, Diastolole! We ca-caught so-something!
OK-K, Systolole!
StarGrazer
HELP!
SOMEONE!

HEY!
Get us out of here!
?!
?
It's ta-talking!
It's mo-moving, too!

OH HO HO! A gu-guy and two ki-kids!
Where are your manners?

We were minding our own business on the deck of our ship and you caught us in your net!
Calm do-down.
It was an accide-dent.

We're fish-ishermen ...
... So of co-course, we fish-ish.
Hee! They talk so funny!
Hee! Hee! Hee!

What do you fish-ish for?
You're so dumb, Sardine!
We fish-ish for st-stars.
Then we se-sell them to the arm-my.
They use them to decorate the sold-diers.
WHAT?!
You're robbing the universe of its beautiful stars in order to decorate your generals?
Well, yeah. It's our jo-job.
They pa-pay us for it.
And who pays you?
President Sup-per . . .
...SUPER-MUSCLE-MAN?
Tha-that's the one!

MEANWHILE, ON THE SPACE STATION "KEEL" . . .
Supermuscleman, sir, I'd like to introduce you to our new commando team, Code Name Whippit. They just graduated from our military academy.

They're specially trained in combat against little children.
Good work, boys!
GLORY TO YOU, SUPERMUSCLEMAN!

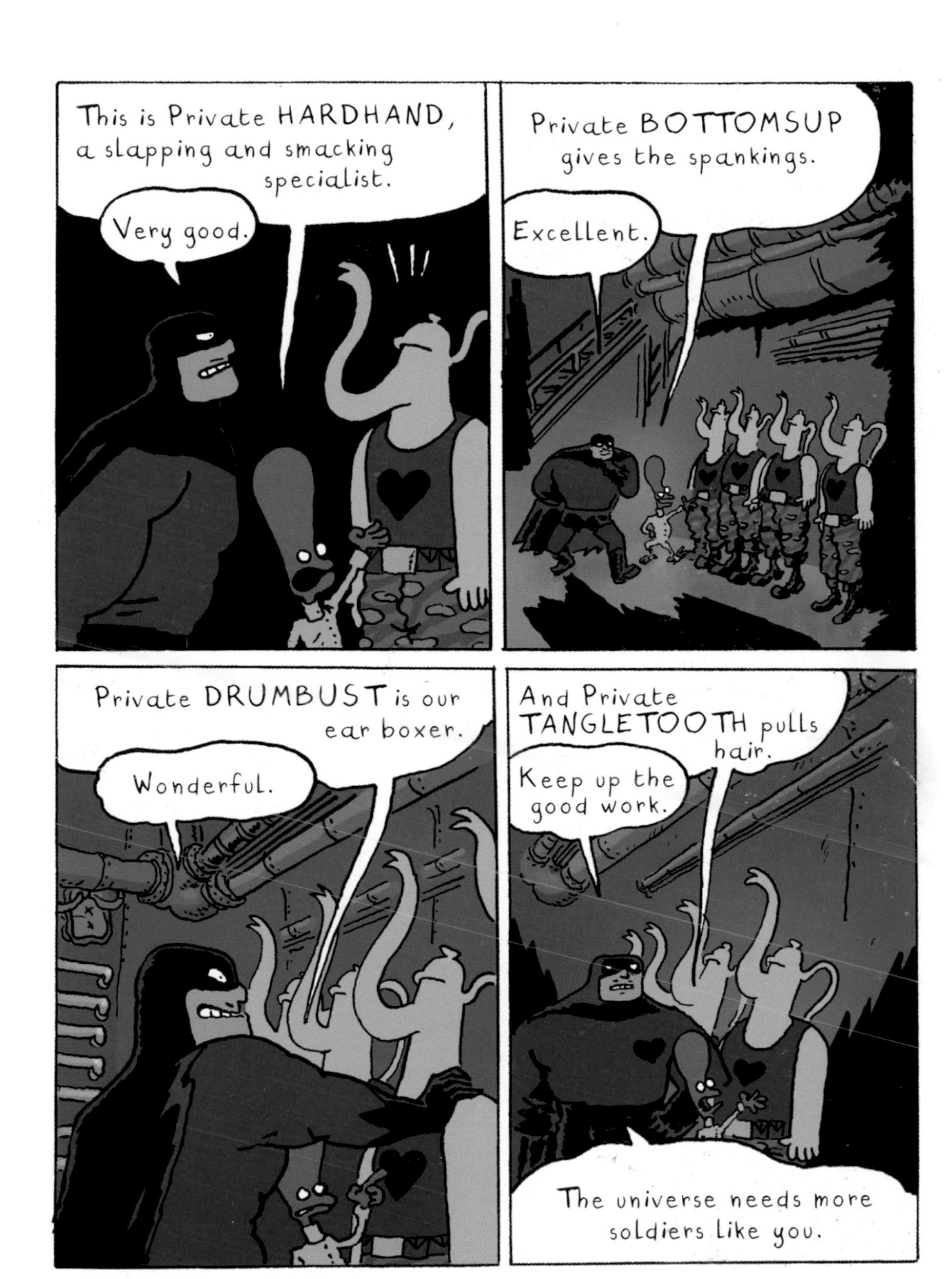
This is Private HARDHAND, a slapping and smacking specialist.
Very good.
Private BOTTOMSUP gives the spankings.
Excellent.
Private DRUMBUST is our ear boxer.
Wonderful.
And Private TANGLETOOTH pulls hair.
Keep up the good work.
The universe needs more soldiers like you.

I am pleased, Krok. Let's decorate these men. Where are the stars?
There are Diastole and Systole with them now.

Hi, boys! Good fishing?
Go-good fish-ishing!
Coo-cool!

Step up to receive your first star, soldiers.

SARDINE!!
Hello-llo!
Hee! Stop it! You're making me laugh too hard!
LITTLE LOUIE!

Let's decorate them in order, starting with the boss!
SMACK!
OUCH!

And the second in command.
OOOPH!
SMACK!

Little children!
ATTACK!
I'll spank the little girl and you pull her hair!
I'll smack the boy and you box his ears!

Come and pick on someone your own size!

PING
PING
PING
Heh! Heh! Heh!
Ha! Ha! Ha!
Hee! Hee! Hee!
Hey!
Oooph!
Ayayay!
Ouch!

WE BEAT THEM, UNCLE YELLOW! Code Name Whippit is down for the count!
Take that! You still want to box my ears?
BING
OUCH! No! That hurts!!
Where'd Supermuscleman and Doc Krok go?
We sa-saw them.
They went tha-that way.
No need to hurry! We'll catch them on their way out!
There's a tra-trap!

Sardine, was it your idea to hang the net outside the door of the KEEL?
Yeah! Just like Diastole and Systole taught us!
This gi-girl is pretty sma-smart.
She'll go fa-far.
Krok, I'm surrounded by idiots and traitors!
Speak up, Supermuscleman. There's a star in my ear!
The End

New York & London

Published by First Second
First Second is an imprint of Roaring Brook Press, a division of Holtzbrinck
Publishing Holdings Limited Partnership
175 Fifth Avenue, New York, NY 10010

Distributed in Canada by H. B. Fenn and Company Ltd.
Distributed in the United Kingdom by Macmillan Children's Books, a division
of Pan Macmillan.

Originally published in France in 2001 under the titles *La machine à laver la cervelle*
and *Les voleurs de yaourts* by Bayard Editions Jeunesse, Paris

Design by Danica Novgorodoff

Library of Congress Cataloging-in-Publication Data

Guibert, Emmanuel.
Sardine in outer space / Emmanuel Guibert and Joann Sfar ; translated by Sasha Watson ;
colorist, Walter Pezzali ; letterer, François Batet.-- 1st American ed.
p. cm.
Translations of stories originally published separately in French.
ISBN-13: 978-1-59643-126-3 (v.1)
ISBN-10: 1-59643-126-1 (v. 1)
ISBN-13: 978-1-59643-127-0 (v. 2)
ISBN-10: 1-59643-127-X (v. 2)

1. Graphic novels. I. Sfar, Joann. II. Title.
PN6747.G85A2 2006
741.5'944--dc22
2005021790

First Second books are available for special promotions and premiums.
For details, contact: Director of Special Markets, Holtzbrinck Publishers.

First American Edition September 2006

Printed in China

1 3 5 7 9 10 8 6 4 2